DOG LOVES DRAWING

LOUISE YATES

RED FOX

Dog loved books!
He loved books
so much that he
had opened
his own
bookshop.

When he wasn't
sharing books with
others, Dog was
reading them
himself.

One morning, a parcel arrived.

Inside was a book,
but as Dog opened
it up, he saw to
his surprise that
it had no words
and no pictures!
"How curious,"
he thought.

Just inside the cover, he noticed a message
from his Aunt Dora that read:

To my dearest Dog,
May the lines you draw open
a door to some wonderful
adventures. With Love from your
Aunt Dora
x x x x

It was a sketchbook!
Dog knew exactly
what to do.

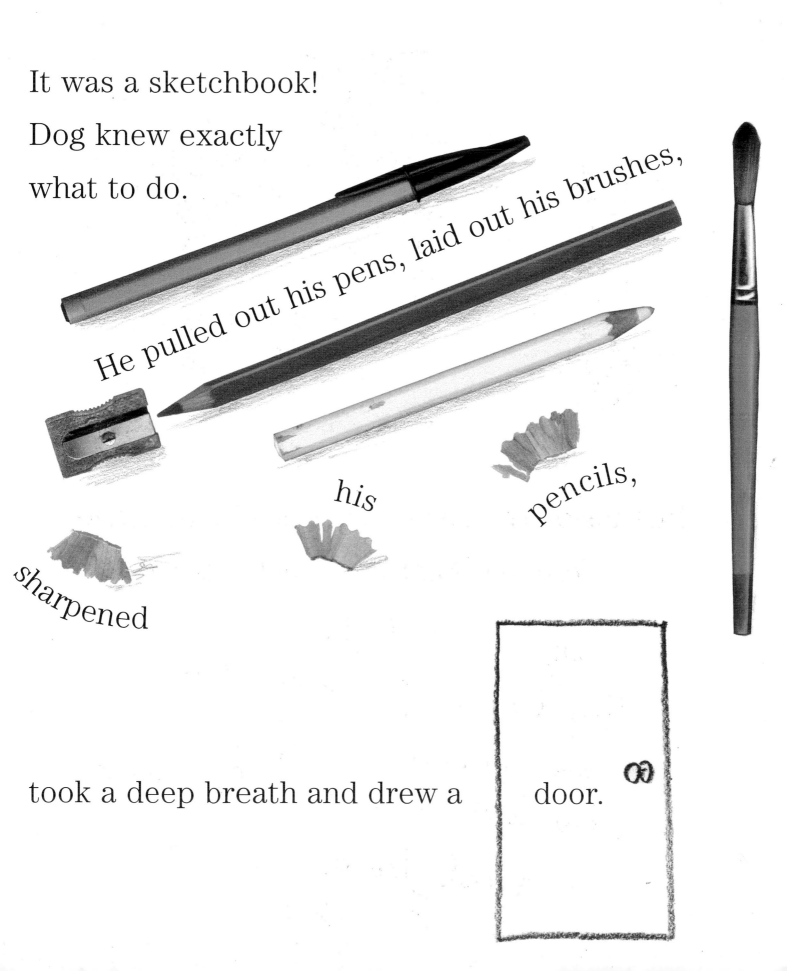

He pulled out his pens, laid out his brushes,

sharpened his pencils,

took a deep breath and drew a door.

He stepped through it,
and on the empty
page in front of him,
Dog drew a stickman.

"Hello," said
the stickman.

"Hello," said Dog.

"I'm not sure what else to draw."

"Let's DOODLE!" suggested the stickman. "That's the best way to come up with ideas." So that is what they did.

Then they turned the page together.

"It would be even more fun
if there were others to join in!"
said Dog. So Dog
drew a duck,

and the duck
drew an owl,
and the owl
drew a crab,
and the crab

did some colouring-in.

Soon they were all spilling on to the . . .

. . . next page.

"What now?" they wondered.

"Let's go on an outing!"
hooted the owl.

So Dog drew a train

and they all climbed aboard.

While the duck was arguing with the
others about who should drive,
the stickman drew himself a driver's hat,

scribbled
some steam,
and . . .

. . . they were off!

The scenery
streaked
past them –
they were
travelling so
FAST!

At last, the stickman drew
the train to a stop.

Dog got out and drew a boat,

while
the crab
scribbled
some sea.

They climbed aboard

(all except the crab, who clung on to the side).

The stickman drew some sandwiches

because he was very hungry.

The owl copied the sandwiches

because she was hungry too,

and the duck drew an enormous cake

because he was the hungriest

of them all!

Dog coloured in a
cloudless sky and
they drifted . . .

The boat drifted a long way

before land appeared.

They all got out and stretched their legs.

The crab drew a parasol to protect himself from the sun.

Then the duck
        decided to draw a . . .

...MONSTER!

And that
spoiled everything.

The monster chased them
all the way round the island
and on to the . . .

. . . next page.

Then Dog had a brilliant idea.

He quickly drew a door

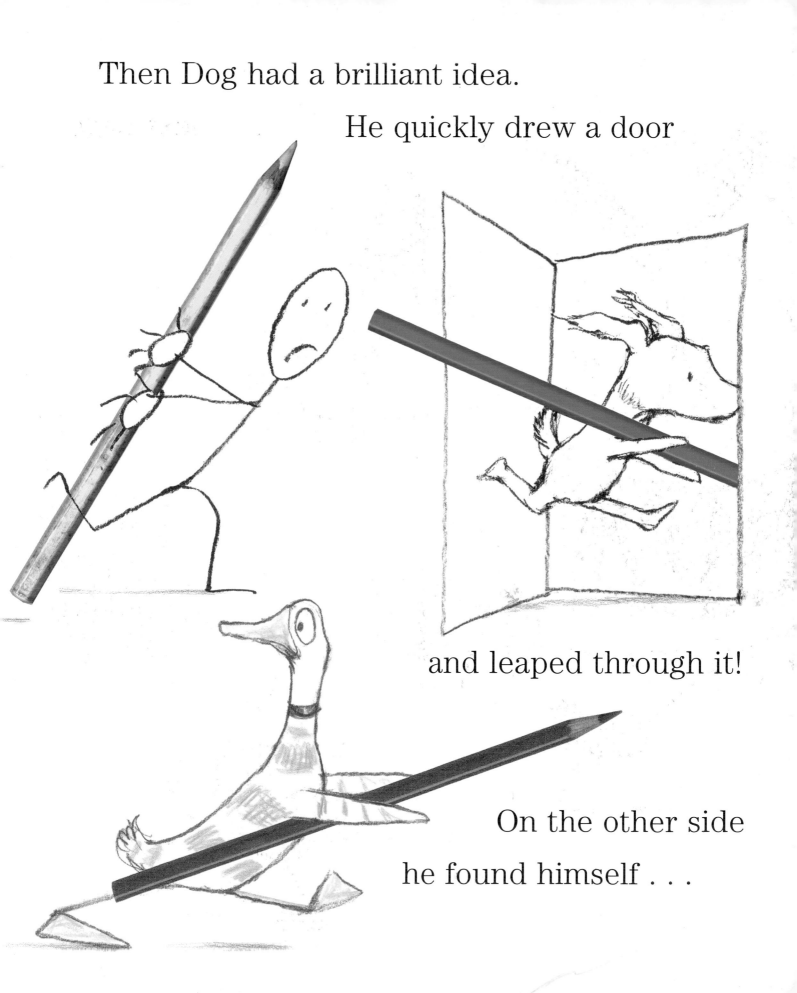

and leaped through it!

On the other side

he found himself . . .

. . . back in
the bookshop!

He turned to the last page of his
sketchbook and made sure that
all his friends were safe and that
the monster could not escape.

KEEP
OUT!

DANGER!

Then he dashed out to
buy some more paper.

Dog loves drawing! And the very next thing he drew was a thank-you card for his Aunt Dora.

For those who taught and encouraged me to draw

DOG LOVES DRAWING
A RED FOX BOOK 978 1 862 30865 7
First published in Great Britain by Jonathan Cape,
an imprint of Random House Children's Books
A Random House Group Company
Jonathan Cape edition published 2012
Red Fox edition published 2012

1 3 5 7 9 10 8 6 4 2

Red Fox Books are published by Random House Children's Books,
61–63 Uxbridge Road, London W5 5SA

www.**kids**at**randomhouse**.co.uk
www.**randomhouse**.co.uk

Addresses for companies within The Random House Group Limited can be found at: www.randomhouse.co.uk/offices.htm
THE RANDOM HOUSE GROUP Limited Reg. No. 954009
A CIP catalogue record for this book is available from the British Library.
Printed and bound in China

The Random House Group Limited supports the Forest Stewardship Council (FSC®), the leading international forest certification organization.
Our books carrying the FSC label are printed on FSC®-certified paper. FSC is the only forest certification scheme endorsed by the leading environmental
organizations, including Greenpeace. Our paper procurement policy can be found at www.randomhouse.co.uk/environment.

MIX
Paper from
responsible sources
FSC
www.fsc.org   FSC® C020056